Growing and Changing

Rachel Sparks Linfield

Series consultant: Julia Stanton

Thanks to the pupils, teachers and parents from St Mary Magdalene
Primary School for taking part in the photo shoots.
Thanks also to Joe Knight and Emma Lewin for lending props.

Thanks are also given to Connie, Rosie and Edmund Linfield and Lucy Field
for trying out creative activities and contributing artwork.

A CIP record for this book is available from the British Library.

ISBN 07136 6808 3

First published 2004 by A & C Black Publishers Limited
37 Soho Square, London W1D 3QZ
www.acblack.com

Text copyright
© 2004 Rachel Sparks Linfield
Illustration copyright
© 2004 Gaynor Berry
Photographs copyright
© 2004 Zul Mukhida
except for Photocard 3 © BarrieWatts;
Photocard 4 © Sally & Richard Greenhill Photo Library

Music copyright:
The following copyright owners have kindly granted their
permission for the reprinting of the words and music:
David Moses for Chicks grow into chickens. Ana Sanderson for
Too big for my boots. Sandra Kerr for A house is a house for me.
Sue Nicholls for Some sounds are short, What is the weather today?,
Make your sound like mine. Scunthorpe & District Teacher's
Centre for Wonderful weather. Jill Darby for Hair.

Printed and bound in China by Leo Paper Products.

A & C Black uses paper produced with elemental chlorine-free pulp,
harvested from managed sustainable forests.

Contents

Introduction

The Foundation Stage begins at three years old, when most children will attend some form of pre-school or nursery. These early years are critical in children's education, and the government's **Early Learning Goals** provide an indication of the skills most children should develop by the end of the Foundation Stage, which is the end of the primary school Reception year.

The Early Learning Goals cover the following areas:

- Personal, social and emotional development
- Communication, language and literacy
- Mathematical development
- Knowledge and understanding of the world
- Physical development
- Creative development

In order to achieve the Early Learning Goals, there are four levels of learning, called **Stepping Stones**. These show the knowledge, skills, understanding and attitudes that children need to develop during the Foundation Stage. Children must show progression through the Stepping Stones in order to achieve the Early Learning Goals.

The Stepping Stones have been colour coded in this pack, in line with the Foundation Stage curriculum. Yellow indicates the expected learning level at the start of the Foundation Stage and grey indicates the expected level at the end of the Foundation Stage.

- YELLOW
- BLUE
- GREEN
- GREY

The Foundations Series

Foundations is a series of activity packs written for all adults working with children at the Foundation Stage across a range of settings: local authority nurseries; nursery centres; playgroups; pre-schools; accredited child minders in approved child minding networks; maintained schools or schools in the independent, private or voluntary sectors.

Each **Foundations** pack contains imaginative activities written specifically for those working with the Early Learning Goals and Stepping Stones. Each activity is tried and tested for suitability with children aged three to five, i.e. children at the Foundation Stage. Each book uses a popular early years theme and contains at least 40 activities that use the theme as a starting point for activities across the six key learning areas. There are also some groups of activities, such as 'Becoming Frogs' on pages 12-13, which encourage children to explore one element within the Growing and Changing theme in more detail.

Growing and Changing contains all you need to plan, organise and successfully lead activities on this theme. The activities are complemented by the following resources:
- a CD of songs, poems and stories, which are integral to the activities
- a giant wall poster, which can be used for display and as a useful stimulus for many of the activities
- eight colour photocards for use with various activities, or as stand alone resources
- photocopiable sheets of resources, practical tasks and games to use with the activities
- ideas for displays and for developing successful links with parents and carers.

Planning and assessment

This pack provides comprehensive coverage of the Early Learning Goals and includes a planning chart to help you organise your teaching. In addition, each activity highlights which Stepping Stones are covered.

During the course of the activities, children should be assessed regularly to ensure that they develop the skills required to progress through the Stepping Stones and achieve the Early Learning Goals. The following tips will help you to plan and compile assessment records for the children.

● Keep planning and assessment records for each of the children you teach. These records can be used at the end of the Foundation Stage to produce a brief report of the child's achievements against the Early Learning Goals and Stepping Stones. The child's next teacher will find this report particularly useful if it includes the themes covered.

● Each activity covers different Stepping Stones. This allows you to choose activities which are at the correct level for the children in your group, and also provides opportunities for assessment by outcome from the activity. Use the Early Learning Goals planning chart (pages 8-9) to ensure you are covering a range of areas of learning.

● Observe what the children do and say while they are working on the activities.

● Talk to them about what they are doing. Ask questions that give the children the opportunity to give open-ended answers, and to suggest what else they might do. You can use the questions suggested with each activity for extra help.

● As part of the assessment process, keep parents and carers informed of the work their child is doing. This pack includes ideas for improving home-school links (pages 32-33) and contains suggestions for activities that can be done at home.

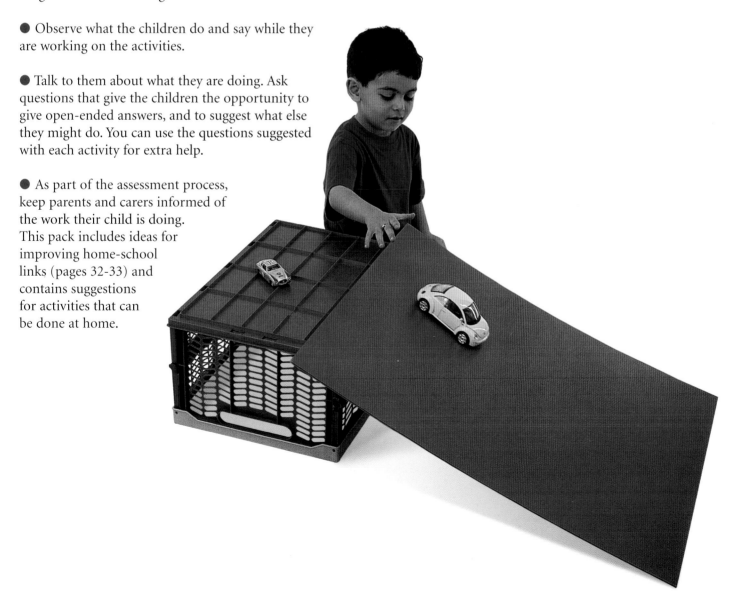

How to use this pack

INTRODUCTION

The text in bold explains the purpose of the activity and outlines some expected outcomes.

INSTRUCTIONS

Follow the step by step instructions to find out how to prepare and carry out the activities.

RESOURCES

This box lists the resources you will need for each activity.

Resources included in the pack are represented by an icon. These could be one of the following:
- Poster
- Activity Sheet
- Photocard
- CD

QUESTIONS

Each activity has a prompt box of questions you could ask the children during the activity.

EXTENSION

Some activities feature a further activity that extends and consolidates the children's understanding of the main activity.

EARLY LEARNING GOALS

This heading indicates the main Early Learning Goal upon which the activity focuses. (See pages 8-9 for other Early Learning Goals which are also covered.)

STEPPING STONES

These are key skills which the activity develops. The colour of the text indicates the corresponding Stepping Stone level in the Foundation Stage curriculum (see page 4).

KEY WORDS

This box contains key vocabulary that the children will encounter in the course of the activity.

Tide times

RESOURCES

Per child, a piece of sand-coloured paper; shiny paper and tissue paper (blue and green); glue; thick black felt pens

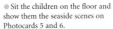
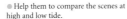
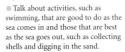

PHOTOCARD 5   PHOTOCARD 6

CREATIVE DEVELOPMENT

Begin to differentiate colours. Use lines to enclose a space, then begin to use these shapes to represent objects. Make collages. Explore colour, texture, shape, form and space in two dimensions.

Key words

tide, sea, in, out, high, low, sand, wave

Introduce the children to the idea of changing tides by making colourful seaside collages.

- Sit the children on the floor and show them the seaside scenes on Photocards 5 and 6.
- Help them to compare the scenes at high and low tide.
- Talk about activities, such as swimming, that are good to do as the sea comes in and those that are best as the sea goes out, such as collecting shells and digging in the sand.
- Ask the children to make a collage of the sea at high tide. Show them how to make waves by sticking overlapping pieces of tissue paper onto the sand-coloured paper, leaving just a small amount of sand.
- Use a black felt pen to draw details, such as a sandcastle.

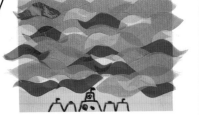

Questions

Have you ever been to the seaside?
What differences can you see in these two photocards?
In which picture can you see the most sand?
What could you do at low tide when there is lots of sand?

Extension

Investigate how to make waves and ripples in a water tray.

Changing weather

RESOURCES

Scissors; brass paper fasteners; crayons

Activity Sheet 4   8-9

KNOWLEDGE AND UNDERSTANDING OF THE WORLD

Talk about what is seen and what is happening. Show an awareness of change. Look closely at similarities, differences, patterns and change.

Key words

sunny, rainy, foggy, windy, cloudy, snowy

This activity encourages children to observe and note down changes in the weather on their own weather boards.

- Photocopy Activity Sheet 4 – one per child.
- Sitting comfortably on the floor, enjoy listening to 'Wonderful weather'.
- Talk about the different types of weather mentioned in the song.

- Hand out the Activity Sheets and ask the children to colour in the sections showing different types of weather.
- Help them to make the activity sheets into weather boards by cutting out the circle and attaching the arrow with a brass paper fastener.
- Listen to 'What is the weather today?' After each verse ask the children to show the weather on their weather boards.

Questions

What is the weather like today?
What colour is the sky?
What was the weather like yesterday?
Which picture will the arrow point to when it is sunny or windy or cloudy?

Extension

Make up new verses for the song 'What is the weather today?'.

16

Growing and Changing

cygnet — swan

puppy — dog

Wall Poster

This giant poster can be used to introduce the topic of Growing and Changing and also provides a useful centrepiece for a display. The words to the songs, stories and poems on the CD are printed on the back of the poster and are accompanied by illustrations. Before putting up the poster, you may wish to enlarge the text on a photocopier for some of the children to follow as they listen to the CD. This will help the children begin to recognise words, even if they cannot 'read' the whole text. The words and illustrations can also be used as part of your display. You may wish to tippex out the track numbers before photocopying the pages.

Photocards

The Photocards can often be used to start an activity and have been chosen to prompt discussion. The questions box offers suggestions of what to ask the children while you are using the Photocards. Try to work with a small group of children so that each picture can be seen clearly. You may also wish to start a collection, adding further photographs and magazine pictures from other sources.

Activity Sheets

Photocopiable Activity Sheets are provided to support particular activities. In some cases, the sheet may be used with a small group, whilst for other activities, each child will need their own copy. The Activity Sheets can be enlarged to A3, copied onto card and laminated so that they last longer. You might also wish to colour in the games.

CD

This CD will play on a CD player or computer with a CD drive and sound facility. Alternatively, you can copy the CD onto an audiotape if you do not have access to a CD player in your setting. The CD includes songs, rhymes, stories, poems and music – all of which are integrated into various activities. Each track is indicated by a numbered CD icon in the resources box. Transcripts of all CD tracks appear on the back of the Growing and Changing poster.

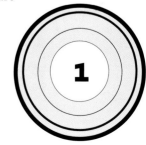

Planning chart

The planning chart below is to help you to plan your coverage of the Early Learning Goals and to enable you to match the activities to the children's ability levels, indicated by the Stepping Stones. Each activity focuses on one main Early Learning Goal (indicated by a black circle in the planning chart) and may also cover secondary Early Learning Goals (indicated by a blank circle). There are two ways in which you may wish to use this chart:

● **Start with the Early Learning Goals and Stepping Stones**
Decide which main Early Learning Goal you would like to cover and at what level (i.e. Stepping Stone). Use the planning chart below to choose an activity that meets your requirements. Refer to the activity page for a more detailed outline of the Stepping Stones covered by the activity. Ensure you keep a record of the Early Learning Goals and Stepping Stones you cover.

● **Start with the activities**
From the chart below, choose an activity that is appropriate for your setting. Keep a record of the Early Learning Goals and Stepping Stones covered by the activity.

Early Learning Goals ➞	Personal, social and emotional development				Communication, language and literacy				Mathematical development				Knowledge and understanding of the world				Physical development				Creative development			
Stepping Stones ➞	YELLOW	BLUE	GREEN	GREY	YELLOW	BLUE	GREEN	GREY	YELLOW	BLUE	GREEN	GREY	YELLOW	BLUE	GREEN	GREY	YELLOW	BLUE	GREEN	GREY	YELLOW	BLUE	GREEN	GREY
Changing trees (p10)	●		●	●									○	○	○	○								
Growing and changing (p10)					●	●	●	●	○	○	○													
Family changes (p11)		●	●	●																		○	○	○
How animals grow (p11)					○	○	○	○						●	●	●								
BECOMING FROGS																								
Eddie's frogspawn (p12)					○	○	○	○					●	●	●	●								
Froggy ponds (p12)																	○	○	○	○	●	●	●	●
Tadpole game (p13)	○	○	○	○					●	●	●	●												
Frog movement (p13)					○	○		○									●	●	●	●				
Growing feet (p14)									●	●	●	●	○		○	○								
Changing words (p14)	○	○	○	○	●	●	●	●																
Writing our names (p15)					●		●	●					○	○	○	○								
Moving house (p15)		●	●	●	○		○	○																
Tide times (p16)																	○	○	○	○	●	●	●	●
Changing weather (p16)													●	●	●						○	○	○	○

Early Learning Goals	Personal, social and emotional development	Communication, language and literacy	Mathematical development	Knowledge and understanding of the world	Physical development	Creative development
Windy weather (p17)				● ● ●	○ ○ ○ ○	
At the weather station (p17)		● ● ● ●				○ ○ ○ ○
HOW PLANTS GROW						
Growing cress (p18)	○ ○ ○ ○			● ● ● ●		
Rosie's carrots (p18)		● ● ●				○ ○ ○ ○
From seed to fruit (p19)			○ ○ ○ ○	● ● ● ●		
Tall flowers (p19)			● ● ● ●			○ ○ ○ ○
Connie's freezing fruits (p20)		● ● ●		○ ○ ○ ○		
Toss a pancake (p20)					● ●	○ ○ ○ ○
Melting chocolate (p21)			● ● ● ●	○ ○ ○ ○		
Dotty snowmen (p21)		○ ○			● ● ● / ● ●	
Making music (p22)				○ ○ ○ ○		● ● ●
Moving pictures (p22)	● ● ●	○ ○				
Mix and match (p23)	○ ○ ○ ○					● ● ● ●
Changing speeds (p23)			○ ○ ○	● ● ● ●		
Recycling paper (p24)				● ● ● ●		
Making models (p24)				● ●		○ ○ ○ ○
Blob pictures (p25)			○ ○ ○ ○			● ● ●
Gigantically tiny (p25)	○ ○ ○			● ● ●		
OUT OF AN EGG						
From egg to animal (p26)		● ● ● ●		○ ○		
Rocking chicks (p26)			○ ○ ○ ○			● ●
The large egg (p27)	○ ○ ○	● ● ● ●				
Clay eggs (p27)				○ ○ ○ ○	● ● ●	
The selfish giant (p28)	● ● ●	○ ○ ○				
How I have grown (p28)	○ ○		● ● ●			
A new hairstyle (p29)			● ● ● ●		○ ○ ○ ○	
New week resolutions (p29)	● ● ●					

9

Changing trees

RESOURCES

Paint; paintbrushes; A3 painting paper; scrap paper; pencils; table covers

PERSONAL, SOCIAL AND EMOTIONAL DEVELOPMENT

Show curiosity. Display high levels of involvement in activities. Be confident to try new activities, initiate ideas and speak in a familiar group.

Key words

winter, spring, summer, autumn

Use the Photocards of the apple trees in winter and summer to encourage the children to talk about how the trees have grown and changed.

- Prepare for the activity by making a summer tree and a winter tree on a display board.
- Show the children the trees on Photocards 1 and 2. Point to the tree in summer and ask for words to describe it.
- Now point to the tree in winter and ask the children to describe it. Compare the summer tree with the winter tree.
- Talk about the seasons. Encourage the children to think about the types of clothes they would wear outside in the summer and in the winter.
- Ask the children to paint self portraits wearing either winter or summer clothes.
- Encourage the children to choose where they would like their portraits to go on the display boards. Ask them to make labels to say 'Winter' and 'Summer'.

Questions

What does this tree look like?
What are on the branches?
What do you like to wear in the winter and in the summer?

Extension

Provide picture books for the children to sort into the seasons in which the stories take place. Remember some stories take place in more than one season!

Growing and changing

RESOURCES

Wax crayons; pencils; A4 clear plastic punched wallets; ribbon or wool; baby clothes and clothes for a 4-5 year old

COMMUNICATION, LANGUAGE AND LITERACY

Draw, sometimes giving meanings to marks. Ascribe meanings to marks. Use writing as a means of recording and communicating. Use phonic knowledge to write simple regular words and make phonetically plausible attempts at complex words.

Key words

baby, child, changing, numbers for ages, growing

Comparing baby clothes with a child's clothes will help the children to understand that they grow and change as they become older.

- Photocopy Activity Sheet 1 – one per child.
- Show the children the baby clothes and compare them with the child's clothes.
- Listen to 'Once I was a baby'. Talk about how the baby changed.

- Encourage the children to think about the things they can do now and the things they hope to do when they are older. Explain that the class is going to make a book to show these things.
- Hand out the Activity Sheets and help the children to complete the sentences. Ask them to illustrate their sentences.
- Place the sheets in the plastic wallets and tie them together to make a class book.

Questions

Who might wear these clothes?
Which top is the longest and which is the shortest?
Do you know a baby? What can he or she do?
What can you do now that you could not do when you were a baby?
What would you like to do when you grow older?

Extension

Invite a new mother to bring her baby into class and give a talk to the children.

Family changes

RESOURCES
Baby-sized doll; doll's clothes; sheets or pieces of fabric

PERSONAL, SOCIAL AND EMOTIONAL DEVELOPMENT

Talk freely about their home and community. Express needs and feelings in appropriate ways. Have a developing awareness of their own needs, views and feelings and be sensitive to the needs, views and feelings of others.

Key words
baby, new, brother, sister, granny

The story 'Poppy's new brother' encourages the children to explore their emotions when a new baby brother or sister is born.

● Ask the children whether they have any younger brothers or sisters. Encourage them to talk about how it feels to have a brother or sister.

● Listen to the story 'Poppy's new brother'. Ask the children to think why Poppy's excitement changed to jealousy when the baby came home.

● Place a baby doll, doll's clothes and sheets in the home corner for groups to role play the story.

Questions
Do you have a baby brother or sister?
Do you help to look after him or her?
Why did Poppy want a new brother?
Why was Poppy cross?

Extension
Ask the children to look through mail order catalogues for pictures of clothes and toys that Poppy's brother might like as a baby and when he is three years old.

How animals grow

RESOURCES

Coloured wax crayons

POSTER
Growing and Changing
cygnet   swan
puppy   dog

Activity Sheet 2

KNOWLEDGE AND UNDERSTANDING OF THE WORLD

Talk about what is seen. Show an awareness of change. Look closely at similarities, differences, patterns and change.

Key words
puppy, dog, swan, cygnet, animal

Help the children learn the names of animal babies and to understand how young animals change and grow.

● Photocopy Activity Sheet 2 – one per child.

● Explain to the children that they are going to listen to a song with lots of animals in it. Encourage them to remember the names of the animals as they listen to 'Chicks grow into chickens'.

● Show the children the poster and ask them to name the animals.

● Encourage them to notice that one of the animal babies changes a lot as it grows older while the other just grows bigger.

● Hand out the Activity Sheets. Ask the children to draw pictures of animal babies that change a lot on one side of the table, and ones that just grow bigger on the other.

Questions
Which animal grows and becomes a sheep/dog/hen or cat?
How many animals can you see?
Which animals do not change a lot and simply grow bigger as they get older?
Which animals change a lot as they grow older?

Extension
Ask the children to look at non-fiction books and magazines to find more animal babies.

BECOMING FROGS

This group of activities introduces the children to the life cycle of a frog and explains the changes that occur as frogspawn develops into tadpoles and tadpoles grow into frogs.

Eddie's frogspawn

RESOURCES

A3 drawing paper; pencils; wax crayons; scissors; sticky tape

KNOWLEDGE AND UNDERSTANDING OF THE WORLD

Show curiosity and interest by facial expression, movement or sound. Describe simple features of objects and events. Examine living things to find out more about them. Find out about, and identify, some features of living things, objects and events they observe.

● Show the children Photocard 3. Point to the frogspawn, tadpoles and frog and explain what they are.

● Listen to the story 'Eddie's frogspawn'.

● Talk about what the story tells us about frogs. Explain that the jelly around the frogspawn keeps the eggs together, protects them and provides food for the tadpoles.

● Make a big picture book of the story 'Eddie's frogspawn'.

Key words

frogspawn, tadpole, frog, tank

Questions

Can you point to a frog?
What colour is the tadpole?
What will the tadpole change into?
What is frogspawn?

Extension

Encourage the children to discover more about the life cycle of a frog by looking at the pictures in non-fiction books.

Froggy ponds

RESOURCES

Per child, a clear plastic container; scissors; bubble wrap; white card; scraps of green paper; blue and green paint (part mixed with PVA glue); stiff brushes; green tissue paper; glue; wax crayons; conkers; grasses

CREATIVE DEVELOPMENT

Begin to differentiate colours. Begin to describe the texture of things. Understand that different media can be combined. Explore colour, texture, shape, form and space in two or three dimensions.

Key words

frogspawn, tadpole, frog, pond, names for materials and colours

● Remind the children of the story 'Eddie's frogspawn'. Explain that they are going to make models of ponds for frogspawn, tadpoles and frogs.

● Talk about the types of things that might be found in a pond.

● Show the children how to use a stiff brush to make splodges of green and blue paint on the inside bottom and sides of the clear plastic container.

● Discuss the materials that can be used to make rocks, plants, frogspawn, tadpoles and frogs. Encourage the children to describe their colours and textures and to suggest ways to use them.

Questions

What could we use to make frogspawn?
Which card would be good for making a tadpole or a frog?
How could we make rocks?
What else could we put in the pond?

Tadpole game

RESOURCES

Per group, one dice. Per child, ten 2 pence coins or white card circles with black dots for frogspawn; coloured pencils

Activity Sheet 3 · SAFETY

Make sure that children do not swallow coins.

MATHEMATICAL DEVELOPMENT

Use mathematical language in play. Willingly attempt to count with some numbers in the correct order. Count an irregular arrangement of up to 10 objects. **Count reliably up to 10 everyday objects.**

Key words

numbers 1-10, frogspawn, tadpole, how many?

● Photocopy Activity Sheet 3 – one per child.

● Put the children into groups of three or four. Hand out the Activity Sheets and ask the children to colour them in.

● Help the children to count the 2 pence coins and to lay them over the tadpoles and baby frogs on the sheet. Explain that the coins are to be frogspawn in the game.

Activity sheet 3

● Ask the children to take it in turns to roll the dice and say the number they have thrown. Ask them to take away the same number of coins (frogspawn) from the Activity Sheet.

● The game finishes when all the coins (frogspawn) have been removed to reveal the tadpoles and baby frogs. During the game, encourage the children to count the number of coins (frogspawn) left.

Questions

How many frogspawn or tadpoles do you have?
How many frogspawn still need to grow into frogs?
Are there more frogspawn or tadpoles?

Extension

Repeat the game with 12 coins. Place the extra ones in spaces on the Activity Sheet. When coins not revealing tadpoles or baby frogs are removed the child misses his or her next go.

Frog movement

RESOURCES

Large area for free movement

 5

PHYSICAL DEVELOPMENT

Respond to a story by means of gesture and movement. Move in a range of ways, such as slithering, shuffling, rolling, jumping, skipping, sliding and hopping. Initiate new combinations of movement and gesture in order to express and respond to ideas and experiences. Move with confidence, imagination and in safety.

Key words

lily pad, frogspawn, tadpole, frog, dot, curve, curl, wriggle, wiggle, tail

● Make sure you are in a large area for free movement. Play 'From frogspawn to frog' and encourage the children to listen carefully.

● Ask the children to curl up into dot shapes. Play 'From frogspawn to frog' again.

● Tell the children that you would like them to pretend to be frogspawn and to change slowly into tadpoles and then into frogs.

Questions

Can you curl into a tiny ball?
Can you wriggle like a tadpole?
Can you do a high jump like a frog?

Growing feet

RESOURCES

Selection of clean shoes in different sizes; chunky wax crayons; plain paper; scissors

6

MATHEMATICAL DEVELOPMENT

Use size language such as 'big' and 'little'. Begin to talk about the shapes of everyday objects. Order two or three items by length. Use language such as 'bigger' to describe the size of solids and flat shapes.

Key words

shoe, size, big, little, shortest, longest

Encourage children to notice the way that feet change and grow and give them the opportunity to compare and order shoes by length.

● Work with a small group of children.

● Talk about going to a shoe shop. Explain why feet need to be measured before buying new shoes.

● Show the children the shoes. As a group compare the lengths and shapes. Ask the children to place the shoes in order of length from the shortest to the longest.

● Show the children how to hold a piece of paper over a shoe sole to make a wax crayon rubbing.

● Ask them to make a rubbing of a shoe that they would like to wear and cut out the shape.

● Enjoy singing the song 'Too big for my boots'.

Questions

Which shoe is the longest?
Which shoe is the shortest?
Who might wear this shoe?
Why do we need shoes in different sizes?
What size shoes do you wear?

Extension

Sponge the soles of a pair of old Wellington boots with paint and walk on large sheets of paper to make footprints.

Changing words

RESOURCES

Per group, cards with b, c, f, m, r, s, at, un, tidy, well, happy and dress written on them

COMMUNICATION, LANGUAGE AND LITERACY

Distinguish one sound from another. Show awareness of rhyme. Hear and say the initial sound in words and know which letters represent some of the sounds. Link sounds to letters, naming and sounding the letters of the alphabet.

Key words

at, change, different, word, untidy, unwell, unhappy, undress

Invite the children to discover how words can be changed by using a different initial sound.

● Work with a small group on the floor.

● Spread out the single letter cards and check that the children can recognise the letters and say their sounds.

● Play 'I spy the letter that begins the word _____.' Encourage the children to give clues as well as spot the sounds.

● Show them the 'at' card. Place the r card at the beginning of the 'at' card and ask them to read the word.

● Encourage the children to change the word by using a different initial sound.

● As a group, make a list of rhyming 'at' words.

● Show the children the 'happy', 'well', 'dress' and 'tidy' cards. Show them how the meanings of the words are changed by adding the prefix 'un'.

Questions

What sound does this letter make?
Which letter would I need to start the word rat?
What happens if I change the r for a p?
How many 'at' words do we have in our list?
What happens if we add 'un' to 'tidy'?
Can you think of any more words that start with 'un'?

Extension

Invite the children to make picture books of 'at' and 'un' words.

Writing our names

RESOURCES
Per child, a piece of blotting or filter paper; bowl; water; washable felt pens (black, green and purple)

COMMUNICATION, LANGUAGE AND LITERACY

Engage in activities requiring hand-eye coordination. Begin to form recognisable letters. Write their own names.

Key words

black, green, purple, move, name

Give children the opportunity to practise writing their names and encourage them to notice the way that letters change when the dyes in felt pens separate out.

● Using felt pens, demonstrate how to write a name in large letters about 1 cm from the bottom of a piece of filter or blotting paper.

● Hold the bottom edge of the paper in a bowl of water making sure that the name does not go in the water.

● Encourage the children to describe the changes that happen as the water travels up the paper leaving a faint name. Help them to describe what happens to the colours.

● Invite the children to try the activity for themselves.

Questions

*What letter begins your first name?
Can you write your name?
How many letters are in your name?
What is happening to the letters?
What is the water doing?*

Moving house

RESOURCES

Per child, a sheet of white A3 paper folded in half; wax crayons; coloured pencils

PERSONAL, SOCIAL AND EMOTIONAL DEVELOPMENT

Talk freely about their home and community. Express needs and feelings in appropriate ways. Have a developing awareness of their own needs, views and feelings and be sensitive to the needs, views and feelings of others.

Key words

moving, house, home, words for homes that children live in

This activity helps the children to consider the changes that occur when they move to a new house.

● Enjoy listening to 'A house is a house for me'.

● Talk about the different kinds of homes that people live in.

● Encourage the children who can remember moving to talk about the changes that took place and how they felt about leaving one home and living in a different one.

● Explain that when people move they have to pack up their belongings.

● Show the children Photocard 4. Encourage them to describe what they see in the van.

● Give each child a piece of A3 paper folded in half.

● Tell the children that the paper is a large crate for moving house. Ask them to draw inside all the things they might need in a new bedroom. Help the children to remember furniture as well as their toys, clothes and books.

Questions

*Where do you live?
Have you ever lived anywhere else?
What did it feel like when you moved house?
If you were to move to a new home what would you need to take to your new bedroom?*

Extension

Use construction toys to build homes. Make 'for sale' signs and posters to advertise the homes.

Tide times

RESOURCES

Per child, a piece of sand-coloured paper; shiny paper and tissue paper (blue and green); glue; thick black felt pens

CREATIVE DEVELOPMENT

Begin to differentiate colours. Use lines to enclose a space, then begin to use these shapes to represent objects. Make collages. Explore colour, texture, shape, form and space in two dimensions.

Key words

tide, sea, in, out, high, low, sand, wave

Introduce the children to the idea of changing tides by making colourful seaside collages.

● Sit the children on the floor and show them the seaside scenes on Photocards 5 and 6.

● Help them to compare the scenes at high and low tide.

● Talk about activities, such as swimming, that are good to do as the sea comes in and those that are best as the sea goes out, such as collecting shells and digging in the sand.

● Ask the children to make a collage of the sea at high tide. Show them how to make waves by sticking overlapping pieces of tissue paper onto the sand-coloured paper, leaving just a small amount of sand.

● Use a black felt pen to draw details, such as a sandcastle.

Questions

Have you ever been to the seaside?
What differences can you see in these two photocards?
In which picture can you see the most sand?
What could you do at low tide when there is lots of sand?

Extension

Investigate how to make waves and ripples in a water tray.

Changing weather

RESOURCES

Scissors; brass paper fasteners; crayons

KNOWLEDGE AND UNDERSTANDING OF THE WORLD

Talk about what is seen and what is happening. Show an awareness of change. Look closely at similarities, differences, patterns and change.

Key words

sunny, rainy, foggy, windy, cloudy, snowy

This activity encourages children to observe and note down changes in the weather on their own weather boards.

● Photocopy Activity Sheet 4 – one per child.

● Sitting comfortably on the floor, enjoy listening to 'Wonderful weather'.

● Talk about the different types of weather mentioned in the song.

● Hand out the Activity Sheets and ask the children to colour in the sections showing different types of weather.

● Help them to make the activity sheets into weather boards by cutting out the circle and attaching the arrow with a brass paper fastener.

● Listen to 'What is the weather today?' After each verse ask the children to show the weather on their weather boards.

Questions

What is the weather like today?
What colour is the sky?
What was the weather like yesterday?
Which picture will the arrow point to when it is sunny or windy or cloudy?

Extension

Make up new verses for the song 'What is the weather today?'.

Windy weather

KNOWLEDGE AND UNDERSTANDING OF THE WORLD

Show an interest in the world in which they live. Comment and ask questions about the natural world. Observe, find out about and identify features in the natural world.

Key words

wind, windy, blow, push, hole, streamer

Watching colourful streamers blowing in the wind will encourage the children to discuss changes in wind direction and strength.

● Prepare for this activity by making each child a card ring from a paper plate.

● Photocopy Activity Sheet 5 to A3 size.

● Hand out the card rings and show the children how to tape or tie long pieces of wool, ribbon and crepe paper to them to make streamers.

● On a windy day, take the rings outside to a safe, open space. Encourage the children to notice the way the wind pulls the streamers and the direction from which the wind blows.

● For one week, record changes in the weather and particularly the strength of the wind on Activity Sheet 5.

Questions

What is wind?
How can we tell if it is a windy day?
What does the wind do to the streamers?
Where is the wind blowing from?
How strong is the wind?

Extension

Invite the children to decorate the plate rings with felt pens. Make a bar chart to show the number of windy days and calm days.

At the weather station

COMMUNICATION, LANGUAGE AND LITERACY

Draw, sometimes giving meanings to marks. Ascribe meanings to marks. Use writing as a means of recording and communicating. Write their own names and other things such as labels and captions.

Key words

sun, rain, fog, wind, cloud, snow, weather station, record, map, symbol, forecast

In this role play activity, the children make weather records and forecasts which reinforce their awareness of changes in the weather.

● Photocopy Activity Sheet 5 – one per child. Photocopy Activity Sheet 6 to A3. Laminate it and cut out the weather symbols.

● Create a weather station. On a table place a telephone, a toy camera, a globe, pencils, an atlas, a book on the weather, the weather symbols and map from Activity Sheet 6.

● Talk to the children about the way the weather is recorded and forecast at a weather station.

● Show the children the map. Invite them to stick on the weather symbols using sticky tack.

● Hand out Activity Sheet 5. Invite pairs of children to play in the weather station. Encourage them to 'write' records and forecasts on their record sheets and to give forecasts on the telephone.

Questions

Which weather symbol shows a sun?
Which one shows rain?
What does this symbol mean?
When are weather forecasts useful?

Extension

Invite the children to make rain gauges from plastic bottles. Record the rainfall over a two week period.

HOW PLANTS GROW

This group of activities introduces children to the different parts of a plant and encourages them to observe the changes that take place as seeds develop into plants.

Growing cress

RESOURCES

Per child, cress seeds and a plastic or polystyrene beaker; kitchen towel; water; magnifiers; teaspoons

KNOWLEDGE AND UNDERSTANDING OF THE WORLD

Explore objects. Talk about what is seen and what is happening. Show an awareness of change. Look closely at similarities, differences, patterns and change.

Key words

cress, seeds, shoot

● Gather together a small group. Shake a packet of cress seeds. Ask the children to describe what they can hear.

● Place a few seeds in a plastic beaker. Hand out magnifiers and ask the group to describe what they can see and smell.

● Give each child a beaker. Show the group how to place a scrunched up piece of paper towel in the beaker to cover the bottom. Help them to wet the paper with teaspoons of water and sprinkle cress seeds on top.

● Place the beakers in a sunny place. Explain to the children that each day they must check to see that the paper is damp and look for any changes in the cress.

Questions

Have you ever eaten cress?
What do these seeds look like?
What will the seeds do?
What happens when the seeds are watered?

Extension

Encourage the children to decorate a larger beaker with wax crayons or stickers. Use this as a plant pot for the beaker of cress.

Rosie's carrots

RESOURCES

Wax crayons; scissors; lolly sticks; sticky tape; picture book of 'Jack and the Beanstalk'

Activity Sheet 7

 10

COMMUNICATION, LANGUAGE AND LITERACY

Respond to simple instructions. Listen to stories with increasing attention and recall. Sustain attentive listening, responding to what they have heard by relevant actions or comments.

Key words

seeds, carrot, root, beanstalk, magical

● Photocopy Activity Sheet 7 – one per child.

● Show the children the pictures in 'Jack and the Beanstalk'. Encourage those who know the story to retell it.

● Introduce Rosie as a child whose favourite story was 'Jack and the Beanstalk'.

● Listen to the story of 'Rosie's Carrots'.

● Hand out Activity Sheet 7. Ask the children to colour in the pictures of Rosie, her parents, the giant carrot and the worm. Help the children to cut out the pictures and tape them to the lolly sticks to make stick puppets.

● Enjoy using the puppets to retell the story of 'Rosie's Carrots'.

Questions

What was Rosie's favourite story?
Which seeds did she plant?
How did Rosie feel when she saw the gigantic carrot?
What happened when Rosie fell into the carrot?

Extension

Encourage the children to make props and scenery for their puppet plays.

From seed to fruit

RESOURCES

Per group, a plastic plant pot filled with potting compost; apple pips; an apple; a knife

PHOTOCARD 1

KNOWLEDGE AND UNDERSTANDING OF THE WORLD

Show curiosity and interest by facial expression, movement or sound. Describe simple features of objects and events. Examine living things to find out more about them. Investigate objects and materials by using all of their senses as appropriate.

Key words

pip, seed, fruit, tree, apple

- Sit a group of children comfortably on the floor.
- Show them the apple and ask them to describe it.
- Cut the apple in half and again ask for descriptive words. Give each child a piece of apple to taste.

- Take out all the pips and ask the children to count them. Explain that the apple pips are seeds that could grow into apple trees.
- Show the children the picture of the tree on Photocard 1 and ask them to describe it
- Involve the children in planting the pips in the plant pot.
- Ask the children to go and wash their hands!

Questions

What kind of fruit is this?
What does this apple look/ feel/ smell and taste like?
How many pips are there in this apple?
What do you think will happen if we plant these apple pips?

Extension

Use a digital camera to record the development of the apple pips into small trees. Help the the children to write labels for the photos. Investigate planting other fruit seeds, such as melon seeds and orange pips.

Tall flowers

RESOURCES

Per child, a sunflower; pieces of blue paper; paper plates; PVA glue; sunflower seeds; yellow paper petals; yellow shiny paper petals; green paper strips and leaves

MATHEMATICAL DEVELOPMENT

Use size language such as 'big' and 'little'. Show interest by sustained construction activity or by talking about shapes or arrangements. Order two items by length or height. Use everyday words to describe position.

Key words

sunflower, petal, stalk, seeds, tallest, shortest, photocard

- Prepare for this activity by growing sunflowers outside, one per child.
- Help the children to measure the height of their sunflower stalk with the strips of green paper.
- Encourage the children to observe the flowers closely and to describe what they see.

- Work with small groups to make sunflower collages. Stick the paper plates onto the blue paper and show the children how to glue the yellow paper petals onto the plate. Stick sunflower seeds in the centre. Add the green paper strips for stalks and green paper leaves.
- Ask the children to point to the tallest and the shortest sunflowers.

Questions

How tall is your sunflower's stalk?
Which sunflower is the shortest and which is the tallest?
Where is your sunflower?

Extension

Show the children a print of Van Gogh's painting 'Sunflowers'. Encourage them to paint a jug of sunflowers.

Connie's freezing fruits

RESOURCES

Access to a freezer; small chunks of honeydew melon; a plastic tray; plastic straws cut in half

COMMUNICATION, LANGUAGE AND LITERACY

Listen to others in small groups when conversation interests them. Listen to stories with increasing attention and recall. Sustain attentive listening, responding to what they have heard by relevant comments, questions or actions.

Key words

freeze, frozen, cold, melon, freezer

Use the story of 'Connie's freezing fruits' to discuss the change that takes place when chunks of melon are frozen to make lollies.

● Before starting, ask the children to wash their hands.

● Listen to the story 'Connie's freezing fruits'.

● Encourage the children to discuss how Connie felt when she discovered there were no lollies in the shop.

● Show the children the melon pieces. Ask them to taste the melon and describe it.

● Remove the skin from the remaining pieces of melon. Push a straw into each piece and place on a tray. Put in a freezer for at least an hour.

● Help the children to compare the lollies with the unfrozen melon.

Questions

Why was Connie excited?
How did she feel when there were no lollies in the shop?
How did Connie make lollies?
What does the melon look, feel and taste like?
What do the melon lollies look, feel and taste like?

Toss a pancake

RESOURCES

small bats; beanbags

PHYSICAL DEVELOPMENT

Show increasing control over an object by touching, pushing, patting or catching it. Use a range of small equipment.

Key words

pancake, mix, stir, fry, toss

Encourage the children to think about the changes that happen when flour, eggs and milk are mixed together to make pancakes.

● Sitting comfortably on the floor, talk about how pancakes are made.

● Mime how to make a pancake, including sieving flour, cracking eggs, pouring in liquid, stirring, frying and tossing.

● Play 'The pancake song'. Encourage the children to join in with the actions and words.

● Take the children outside. In a safe, open space use the bats as frying pans and the beanbags as pancakes to play toss a pancake.

Questions

Have you ever eaten a pancake?
How are pancakes made?
How many times can you toss your pancake?

Extension

Invite small groups of children to help you make real pancakes.

Melting chocolate

MATHEMATICAL DEVELOPMENT

Show an interest in numbers and counting. Recognise groups with one, two or three objects. Count out up to six objects from a larger group. Count reliably up to 10 everyday objects.

Key words

numbers 1-10, sweet, chocolate, melt, runny, solid

Introduce the children to the reversible change of melting chocolate and give them the opportunity to practise counting up to ten.

● Photocopy Activity Sheet 8 – one per child.

● Work with a pair of children. Ask them to wash their hands before starting.

● Melt 50g chocolate over a bowl of warm water or in a microwave oven.

● Show the children the melted chocolate and ask them to compare it with a square of solid chocolate.

● Ask the children to take it in turn to place a teaspoon of melted chocolate into a petit-four case.

● Ask them to count out one, two, three or four sweets and place them in the melted chocolate. Leave the chocolate to cool and become solid again.

● Encourage the children to make a record of melting the chocolate by sequencing the pictures on Activity Sheet 8.

Questions

What has happened to this chocolate?
Why did the chocolate melt?
What will happen to the melted chocolate?
How many sweets are in this case?
Can you think of other things like chocolate that can change and then change back again?

Extension

Encourage the children to count how many sweets have been used altogether.

Dotty snowmen

PHYSICAL DEVELOPMENT

Engage in activities requiring hand-eye coordination. Demonstrate increasing skill and control in the use of mark-making implements. Manage body to create intended movements. Demonstrate the control necessary to hold a shape or fixed position. Move with control and coordination.

Key words

water, ice, melt

Asking the children to mime making a snowman that melts in the sun will reinforce their understanding of melting and freezing.

● Photocopy Activity Sheet 9 – one per child.

● Show a small group the photograph of the snowman on Photocard 7. Talk about the times of year when a snowman could be made.

Activity sheet 9

● Ask the children to mime making a snowman.

● Hand out the Activity Sheets. Ask the children to join up the dots in the first picture to draw a snowman.

● Explain that when the sun comes out the snowman will melt.

● Ask the children to mime the snowman melting.

● Complete the activity sheet and colour in.

Questions

What is in this photograph?
Have you ever seen or made a snowman?
What happens to snow when the sun comes out?

Extension

Freeze a large block of ice in a plastic tub. See how long it takes to melt completely. (Children should not touch the ice with their bare hands.)

Making music

CREATIVE DEVELOPMENT

Show an interest in the way musical instruments sound. Explore and learn how sounds can be changed. Recognise and explore how sounds can be changed.

Key words

short, long, quiet, loud, high, low, sound, names for instruments used

Try playing a variety of musical instruments to explore how sounds can be changed, then make your own pencil xylophones.

● Prepare for this activity by making each child a frame from stiff card, as shown in the photo.

● Ask four children to choose percussion instruments to use while listening to 'Some sounds are short' and 'Make your sound like mine'.

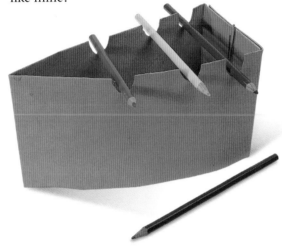

● Talk about how sounds made by the instruments can be changed.

● Show the children the card frames. Lay the coloured pencils on top and tap them with the pencil beater.

● Encourage the children to enjoy playing the pencil xylophones and to discover that the shortest pencil makes the highest note.

Questions

What is this instrument called?
Can you play it quietly and loudly?
If I hit this triangle how can I make the sound stop?
What is the difference between these two sounds?

Extension

Challenge the children to find pencils that can be tapped to play the first line of 'Mary had a little lamb'. Make pencil xylophones with more notes.

Moving pictures

Activity Sheet 10

PERSONAL, SOCIAL AND EMOTIONAL DEVELOPMENT

Show curiosity. Display high levels of involvement in activities. Be confident to try new activities.

Key words

skip, up, down

This activity is based on a 'flip book' optical illusion in which a picture appears to change when the pages are flipped through rapidly.

● Photocopy Activity Sheet 10. Colour in the pictures. Cut along the dotted lines and place the drawings together so that the flowers are exactly on top of one another. Tape the drawings together on the left-hand side.

● Show the children the cartoon video box. Explain that cartoons are made up of many pictures that change a little at a time.

● Show them the taped-together drawings and point out the differences in the pictures.

● Hold a pencil at the right-hand edge of the top picture. Roll the picture around the pencil as far as it will go. Move the pencil forwards and backwards quickly so that the picture is rolled and unrolled rapidly. The child will smile and wink as she skips. The butterfly's antennae will move up and down.

● Give each child a piece of white paper, 10 x 30 cm, folded in half. Encourage the children to make their own changing pictures.

Questions

Have you ever seen this video?
What changes do you see as I move the top picture?
What sort of things could you draw in your changing picture?

Mix and match

RESOURCES

Crayons; felt pens; pencils; scissors

Activity Sheet
11

CREATIVE DEVELOPMENT

Begin to differentiate colours. Use lines to enclose a space, then begin to use these shapes to represent objects. Make drawings. Explore colour, shape, form and space in two dimensions.

Key words

head, hair, body, arm, leg, names of colours

This simple mix and match game encourages children to collaborate as they make a variety of animals and people with changing body parts.

● Photocopy Activity sheet 11 onto card – one per child.

● Hand out the Activity Sheets and show the children the head, body and legs.

● Ask them to draw and colour an animal or a person on the Activity Sheet. Explain that the head, body and legs must be in the same place as the shapes shown in dots. Encourage the children to add arms, tails and other features.

● Help the children to cut their animal or person into three rectangles to give a body, head and legs.

● As a group, use different rectangles to make a variety of changing animals and people. Explain to the children that people are animals too.

Questions

What have you drawn?
How many eyes does your animal or person have?
What shall we call this animal or person?

Changing speeds

RESOURCES

A large and a small toy car; a ramp

KNOWLEDGE AND UNDERSTANDING OF THE WORLD

Explore objects. Talk about what is seen and what is happening. Show an awareness of change. Look closely at similarities, differences, patterns and change.

Key words

ramp, high, low, steep, slope, fast, slow, further, furthest

Observe how different-sized toy cars change speed as they travel down ramps placed at varying heights.

● Work outside or in a large, open space.

● Set up the ramp and show the children the toy cars.

● Ask them to predict what will happen when the toy cars are released down the ramp.

● Talk about what the children observe.

● Encourage the children to alter the height of the ramp to vary the speeds of the cars and the distances the cars travel.

Questions

What will happen when I let go of this car?
How could I make the car go faster or slower?
How could I make the car go further?
Which car will go the furthest?

Tip – ramps can be made from stiff card raised by plastic crates, books, or from pieces of clean, plastic guttering.

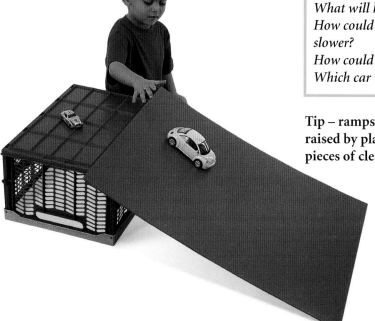

Recycling paper

KNOWLEDGE AND UNDERSTANDING OF THE WORLD

Show an interest in why things happen and how things work. Talk about what is seen and what is happening. Show an awareness of change. Ask questions about why things happen and how things work.

Key words

recycle, newspaper, card

Teach children about recycling and give them the opportunity to notice the changes that occur as they recycle newspaper to make card.

● Ask the children to help tear up eight sheets of newspaper into small pieces and place in a large plastic container.

● Add four cups of water. (More may be needed, depending on how absorbent the paper is.)

● Working with pairs of children, show them how to pulp the paper by pulling it apart in the water.

● Encourage the children to notice the changes that take place as the dye comes out, the paper becomes fluffy and the print is no longer readable.

● Drain the pulp in a sieve. Spread it out on to the plastic margarine lids and press it in firmly. Leave to dry in a sunny area.

● Each day examine the pulp. Within a week it should have dried into sheets of rough cardboard.

Questions

What does the pulp look like?
What does recycling mean?
How could we use our recycled card?
What else can be recycled?

Extension

Invite the children to use the recycled card to make pictures.

Making models

KNOWLEDGE AND UNDERSTANDING OF THE WORLD

Construct with a purpose in mind, using a variety of resources. Build and construct with a wide range of objects, selecting appropriate resources, and adapting their work where necessary.

Key words

bottle, masking tape

Invite the children to observe how appearances can be changed by painting and decorating plastic bottles to make a variety of different models.

● Prepare for this activity by placing a little sand in each bottle to make it stable. Fasten the lids tightly!

● Show the children the plastic bottles. Explain that they can be changed to make models.

● Ask the children to think of ways that the bottles could be used.

● Explain that plastic must be covered with strips of masking tape if it is to be painted.

● Encourage the children to select the items they need to make their models and to enjoy designing and making.

Questions

What could we make using a bottle?
How could you turn it into a robot, a rocket, a teddy bear or a train?
Why is there sand in this bottle?

Extension

Invite the children to bring in and show 'Transformers' – toys that can be changed from one shape into another.

Blob pictures

RESOURCES

Per child, a large circle of black card; runny paint (red, yellow, blue and white); large box lined with newspaper; thick paintbrushes; painting aprons; scrap paper

CREATIVE DEVELOPMENT

Begin to differentiate colours. Explore what happens when mixing colours. Explore colour, texture, shape, form and space in two dimensions.

Key words

blob, down, across, run, mix, words for colours

This painting activity encourages the children to notice the changes that happen when different colours are mixed together.

● Prepare the paint so that it is runny enough to travel slowly down a piece of paper held vertically and thin enough to mix with other paints.

● Demonstrate how to make a blob picture. Place blobs of paint on a circle of black card and hold it vertically in the box (to catch drips). As blobs approach the edge, turn the circle to change the directions in which the blobs move.

● Give each child a circle of black card and encourage them to make their own blob pictures. Ask them to describe the patterns and colours that they make.

Questions

What will happen to a blob of paint placed on this card?
What will happen when the red paint meets the white?
What does this pattern look like?

Gigantically tiny

RESOURCES

Plastic magnifiers; pencils; plain paper

PHOTOCARD

8

KNOWLEDGE AND UNDERSTANDING OF THE WORLD

Show an interest in the world in which they live. Comment and ask questions about where they live and the natural world. Observe, find out about and identify features in the place they live and the natural world.

Key words

thumb print, brick, leaf vein, orange, magnifier, magnified

Provide children with a practical opportunity to experience growing and changing by examining magnified images.

● Show the children Photocard 8. Explain that the pictures show magnified sections of objects.

● Ask the children to say what they think the photographs show and why.

● Take small groups outside. Provide magnifiers for the children to look at a variety of natural and man-made objects.

● Back inside, encourage the children to look at their hands through magnifiers and to draw the patterns they see.

Questions

What does this photo show?
What happens when we look through a magnifier?
What can you see on your hand?

Extension

Invite the children to use a microscope to observe torn paper.

OUT OF AN EGG

This group of activities helps children to understand that some animals hatch out of eggs and encourages them to think about the changes that take place as the animals grow.

From egg to animal

RESOURCES

Wax crayons; non-fiction big book; scissors; glue sticks; egg-shaped pieces of paper; stapler

Activity
Sheet

12

COMMUNICATION, LANGUAGE AND LITERACY

Show interest in print and illustrations in books. Handle books carefully. Enjoy an increasing range of books. **Read a range of familiar and common words independently.**

Key words

egg, duck, snail, fish, crocodile, turtle, snake

● Photocopy Activity Sheet 12 – one per child.

● Show the children the non-fiction big book.

● Look at features, such as the title, page numbers and illustrations. Ask the children to point out letters and words that they recognise.

● Show the children Activity Sheet 12 and help them to identify the animals.

● Explain that the pictures can be used to make a book about animals that hatch out of eggs.

● Hand out the Activity Sheets. Ask the children to colour in the animals and help them to cut out the shapes. Stick the animals onto the egg-shaped pieces of paper and staple together on the left-hand edge to make a book.

● Encourage the children to add words and simple sentences about the animals.

Questions

Where is the snake?
What sound does the word snake start with?
Which animal starts with a 't'?
What is this animal?

Extension

Encourage the children to use non-fiction books to find more animals that come from eggs.

Rocking chicks

RESOURCES

Card (white and orange); crayons; glue; paper scraps; scissors

Activity
Sheet

13

CREATIVE DEVELOPMENT

Make collages. Work creatively on a small scale. Explore shape, form and space in two dimensions.

Key words

rocking, chick, egg, nest

● Prepare for the activity by photocopying the templates on Activity Sheet 13 onto card.

● Cut the rocker from orange card and the egg, chick's head, body, wing and beak from white card. Cut out enough card pieces for each child to make a rocking chick and an egg.

● Show the children how to fold the orange circle in half to make the rocker and demonstrate how it rocks.

● Give each child the pieces to make a chick and an egg and ask them to decorate them with crayons.

● Ask the children to stick a chick on to one side of the orange rocker and an egg on the other side. Ask them to draw a nest around the egg.

● Ask the children to time how long they can make the chick rock.

Questions

What shape is this?
Can you make a chick from these shapes?
Which shapes will you use?

The large egg

POSTER
Growing and Changing

cygnet   swan

puppy   dog

15

COMMUNICATION, LANGUAGE AND LITERACY

Draw and paint, sometimes giving meanings to marks. Ascribe meanings to marks. Use writing as a means of recording and communicating. **Write their own names and other things such as labels and captions and begin to form simple sentences, sometimes using punctuation.**

Key words

swan, duck, duckling, river, cygnet

● Listen to the story of 'The large egg'.

● Talk about the story and discuss the feelings of the different birds.

● Show the children the pictures of the swan and the cygnet on the Poster and ask them to describe what they see.

● Ask the children to paint a picture to show a favourite part of the story.

● When the paintings are dry, help the children to write captions and name labels for their pictures.

Questions

Why did the large duckling feel sad?
How did the mother feel at the start of the story?
Why did the mother duck's feelings change?
What does this poster show?

Clay eggs

PHYSICAL DEVELOPMENT

Use one-handed tools and equipment. Explore malleable materials by patting, stroking, poking, squeezing, pinching and twisting them. **Handle malleable materials safely and with increasing control.**

Key words

clay, dough, soft, hard

● Prepare for this activity by taking small groups of children on walks to collect small sticks, leaves, stones and other natural materials.

● Make an egg out of clay. Show it to the children and explain that it is about to hatch.

● Gently shape the clay to make an imaginary or real animal.

● Decorate it with things the children found on their walks.

● Ask the children to think of a name for the animal, and discuss where it lives and what it eats. Encourage the children to make and decorate their own clay animals.

● Leave the finished animals to harden.

Questions

What might this animal be called?
Where might it live?
What does it like to eat?

Extension

Help the children to describe the changes that occur as the clay hardens.

The selfish giant

RESOURCES

crayons; notice saying 'Stay out, children not wanted'

Activity Sheet 14 / 16

PERSONAL, SOCIAL AND EMOTIONAL DEVELOPMENT

Have a sense of belonging. Express needs and feelings in appropriate ways. Have a developing awareness of their own needs, views and feelings and be sensitive to the needs, views and feelings of others.

Key words

garden, selfish, giant, lonely

Use the story of 'The selfish giant' to stimulate a discussion about feelings and how and why they can change.

● Sitting comfortably on the floor, listen to the story of 'The Selfish Giant'.

● Show the children the notice. Together cross out 'out' and 'not'. Read the new notice.

● Encourage the children to think about how the giant changed and discuss the feelings of the children in the story when they could not play in the garden.

● Show the children Activity Sheet 14. Talk about the differences between the gardens. How many changes can they spot?

Questions

Why did the giant not want to share his garden?
How did the children feel when they could not play in the garden?
What helped the giant to change his mind?

Extension

Encourage the children to colour the pictures of the gardens and to tell stories about the pictures.

How I have grown

RESOURCES

Timeline made from a frieze or wallpaper; pencils; wax crayons; glue; scissors

1

MATHEMATICAL DEVELOPMENT

Show an interest in numbers and counting. Willingly attempt to count with some numbers in the correct order. Recognise numerals 1-5.

Key words

once, now, grown, changed, numbers 1-5

Encourage the children to collaborate to make a timeline and to think about how they have grown and changed since they were babies.

● Prepare for the activity by making a timeline with the numbers 0, 1, 2, 3, 4 and 5 written clearly at 30 cm intervals. Ask parents and carers to show their children photographs (if available) of the children as babies, toddlers and now.

● Listen to 'Once I was a baby' and ask the children to talk about how they have changed since they were babies.

● Show the children the timeline. Ask them to draw pictures to show what they looked like when they were babies and at other ages.

● Encourage the children to cut out their pictures and to stick them on to the timeline at the appropriate points.

Questions

What did you look like when you were a baby?
What do you look like now?
How have you changed?

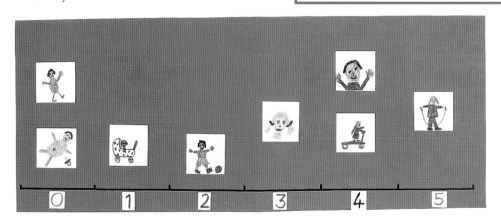

A new hairstyle

MATHEMATICAL DEVELOPMENT

Use size language such as 'big' and 'little.' Show interest by sustained construction activity or by talking about shapes or arrangements. Order two or three items by length. Use language such as 'greater' or 'smaller' to compare quantities.

Key words

hair, long, short, curly, straight

Designing different hairstyles with paper hair will encourage the children to focus on ways we can change the way we look.

● Prepare for the activity by stapling ten strips of black paper 'hair' to each side of a paper plate. Make one plate per child.

● Listen to the song 'Hair' and talk about the different types of hair mentioned.

● Tell the children that you have some friends who have very similar hair. Ask the children to help them to look different by designing new hairstyles.

● Give each child a plate with the 'hair' attached. Explain that the hair can be cut. Show them the materials that can be used to add decorations or a fringe.

● Encourage the children to invent new styles and to describe the changes that they make.

● Ask the children to describe to each other the hairstyles they have created.

Questions

How long is your hair?
Have you ever had longer or shorter hair?
How could we change the style of this paper hair?
Where could we put a bow?

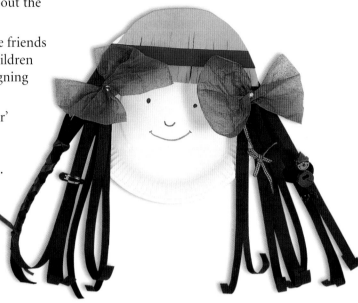

New week resolutions

PERSONAL, SOCIAL AND EMOTIONAL DEVELOPMENT

Feel safe and secure and demonstrate a sense of trust. Value and contribute to own well-being and self-control. Work as part of a group or class, taking turns and sharing fairly, understanding that there needs to be agreed values and codes of behaviour for groups of people, including adults and children, to work together harmoniously.

Key words

change, different

Use this activity to complete the 'Growing and Changing' topic and to encourage the children to think of changes they can make to help others.

● Ask the children to suggest ways they should behave when someone is talking to them. Talk to the children about 'listening eyes' that look at the person who is speaking.

● Talk about the variety of activities they have carried out during the topic on growing and changing. Talk about the things they enjoyed and those that they might wish to have changed.

● Listen to 'Sometimes'. Ask the children to think about the things they might do in the coming week and whether there is anything that they could change to make people feel happier.

● As a group, make a list of 'New Week Resolutions'.

Questions

Which activities have you enjoyed?
What could you have changed?
What did the person in the poem like to do?
Are there changes that we could make that would help us all to feel happier?

Display ideas

Displays can be used to stimulate interest in a topic or to reinforce an idea or skill. Displays of children's work can add value to what they have done, raise self-esteem and help them learn to share. Good displays can lead to a stimulating environment and give great pleasure, both to the children who create the displays and to the parents and carers who come to admire them. The following display suggestions make use of the activities and resources in this pack.

Display tips
● Wallpapers make long-lasting backgrounds that do not fade as quickly as sugar papers.
● Corrugated card helps to provide 3-D parts to flat displays. It is particularly useful for trees and logs.
● Borders around displays help to focus eyes on the display contents.
● Ceilings, cupboards and windows are valuable display areas.
● PVA glue mixed with water makes a good varnish for models and collages.
● Hairspray is good for fixing chalk and pastel pictures.

Changing trees (see page 10)

● Cover the top half of a large board with sky blue wallpaper, half the ground area with grass green sugar paper, to represent summer, and the remaining area with grey sugar paper, to represent winter.

● Cut two identical apple tree trunks and branches from brown textured paper. Stick one tree onto the green paper and the other tree onto the grey paper.

● Make leaves for one tree by sponging green paint onto leaves and printing onto light green sugar paper. When dry, cut out the leaves and staple them loosely to the branches of the tree standing on the green paper.

● Cut out portraits of the children in summer and winter clothes. Stick them on black sugar paper and cut out leaving a narrow black border.

● Encourage the children to identify the summer and winter trees and to choose where they would like their portraits to be displayed.

● Make labels to say 'Summer' and 'Winter'.

Summer

Winter

Blob pictures (see page 25)

- Cover a board with grey sugar paper.

- Make a black border and stick it around the edge of the backing paper.

- Stick on the blob pictures to look like planets in outer space. For a 3-D effect, glue some of the circles onto small boxes before displaying them in grey space.

- Provide sticky stars for children to enjoy sticking on the grey backing paper.

Out of an egg (see pages 26-27)

- Cut a large egg shape from stiff card. Cut it into two pieces leaving a jagged edge. Involve the children in covering the egg with pieces of clean eggshell stuck down with PVA glue.

- Cover a large board with black paper. Stick the two pieces of egg in the centre with the words 'Out of an egg' appearing to come out of the broken egg.

- Around the egg display the children's paintings for 'The large egg' story.

- Cover a nearby table with blue cloth. Arrange the rocking chicks and clay eggs on the table. Ask the children to make labels that say 'Please look but do not touch'.

- In a box, place books that have pictures of animals hatching out of eggs.

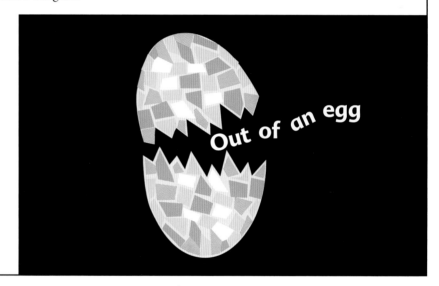

Tall flowers (see page 19)

- Cover a large board with sky blue wallpaper. Use black sugar paper for soil.

- Ask the children to sponge print grey paint over the black paper to give a textured effect.

- Put a red, yellow or orange border around the board – ask the children to decide which colour would look best.

- Display the plate sunflowers in height order. Involve the children in working out where their sunflowers should be placed.

- Ask the children to help make name labels for the sunflowers.

- Put some seeds in see-through sealed containers. Leave on a table with some magnifiers.

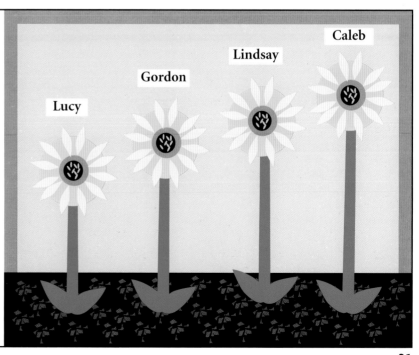

Working with parents and carers

Each time you begin a new topic with the children, remember to pass this information to their parents or carers. You can do this by putting a notice on the parent and carer board, telling them what the current topic is. Alternatively, you can send a letter home to explain which themes will be covered. The letter can give parents and carers ideas for activities they can do at home, both to extend their child's learning and to help the child make connections between home and the classroom.

You might want to use the letter below as a template:

Dear Parents,

Our topic from .... to .... is Growing and Changing.

This topic helps children to become more aware of the way things grow and change in the world around them. As part of the topic, children will be able to watch plants grow, to look at changes that take place during cooking and to think about the way they grow and change. If you have photos of family members that show how they have grown and changed, it would be lovely if you could share these with your children. We will be doing a number of creative activities. If you have any bubble wrap, clean plastic bottles, clear plastic boxes or ice-cream tubs that you no longer need, we would love to receive them.

We would also like to invite you to come and see the displays that the children will be helping to make.

Yours sincerely,

On the next page we have provided some simple activities that can be carried out at home to support the children's understanding of the 'Growing and Changing' topic. Each one is designed to be done after the school activities have been completed, and uses items easily found around the house. You may want to photocopy the page, and add dates to show when you will cover the activity in class, before sending it home. Parents and carers may wish to ask you questions or make comments about the activities they have tried at home. Such discussion will make them feel more involved in their child's development and more willing to continue the 'at-home' activities.

We shall be covering the following activities over the next few weeks as part of the topic 'Growing and Changing'. You may wish to try some of the related activities once we have covered the main activity in class in order to reinforce your child's learning.

GROWING AND CHANGING ACTIVITY IDEAS

Activity: Growing and changing _____
- Collect pictures from cards, seed catalogues and magazines to make a book of things that grow and change.
- Enjoy sharing photos of family members with your child to show how people change and grow.

Activity: Eddie's frogspawn _____
- Make tadpoles by stuffing old black socks with tissue paper. Use bubble wrap as frogspawn.
- Together, make up stories about the tadpoles and the frogs they might become one day.

Activity: Changing weather _____
- For a week, listen to or watch the weather forecast. Before bedtime each day talk to your child about the accuracy of the forecast. Were there any differences in the actual weather?
- Blow bubbles outside. Watch how the wind makes them move.

Activity: Growing feet _____
- Visit a shoe shop. Look for the numbers and sizes written in the shoes.
- Watch to see how feet are measured.
- Back home, make shoes for a doll or teddy with paper and tape.

Activity: Rosie's carrots _____
- Cut the top from a leafy carrot. Leave it to grow on a saucer of water.

Activity: Connie's freezing fruits _____
- Investigate what pieces of banana taste like when frozen.
- Dip the frozen pieces in melted chocolate .
- Encourage your child to notice what happens to the chocolate.

Activity: Making music _____
- Use boxes, tubes, tins etc to make a musical instrument.
- How many sounds can it make? Can the sounds be changed?

Activity: Making models _____
- Collect clean plastic bottles. How many different ones can be found?
- Use them for model making. How can the bottles be changed?

Activity: Out of an egg _____
- Use broken, clean pieces of egg shell to make a collage of something that grows.
- When completed, paint the collage with paint mixed with PVA glue.

Activity: The selfish giant _____
- Make model gardens in plastic tubs for a Selfish Giant.
- Use small twigs and fir cones for trees and moss for hills. Include a pond or stream.

When I am ..... I will...

I am ...... years old. I can ....

Animals that change a lot	Animals that just grow bigger

Foundations **Growing and Changing** A & C Black

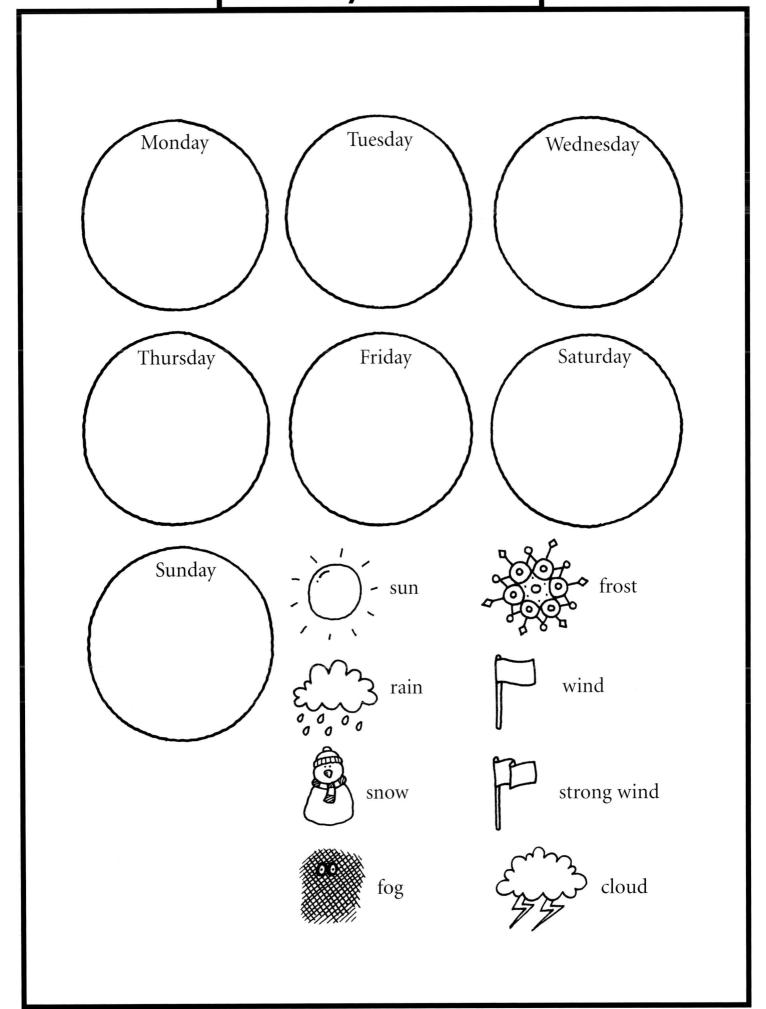

Monday

Tuesday

Wednesday

Thursday

Friday

Saturday

Sunday

sun

frost

rain

wind

snow

strong wind

fog

cloud

Foundations   **Growing and Changing**   A & C Black

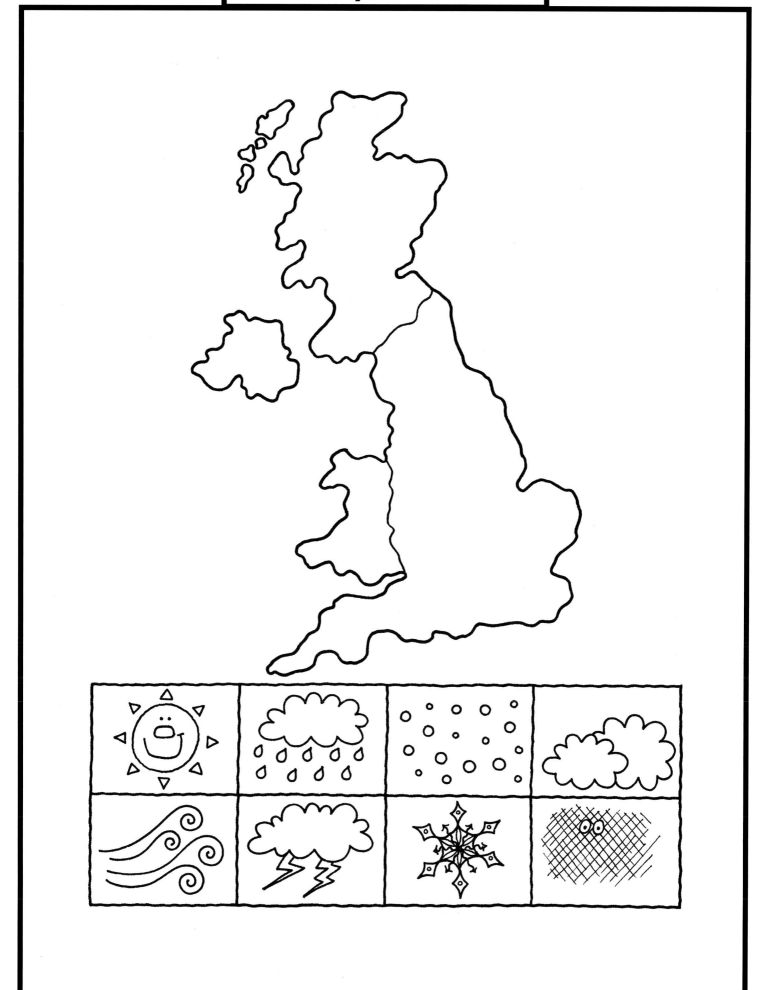

Foundations   **Growing and Changing**   A & C Black

Activity sheet 8

Foundations   **Growing and Changing**   A & C Black

cut

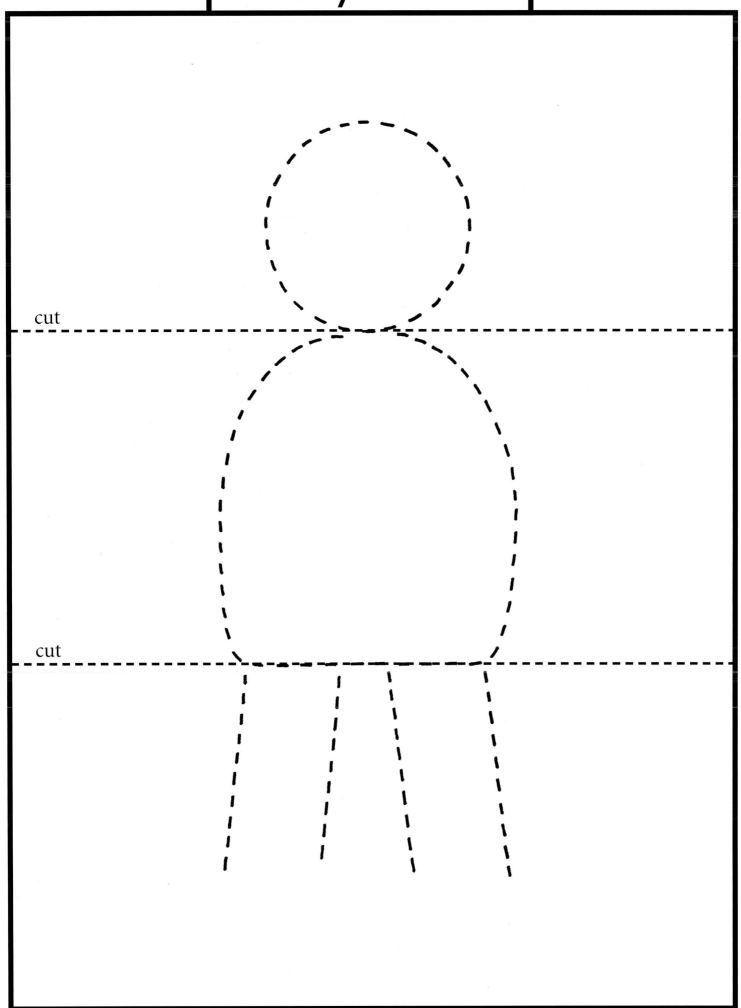

cut

cut

Activity sheet 13

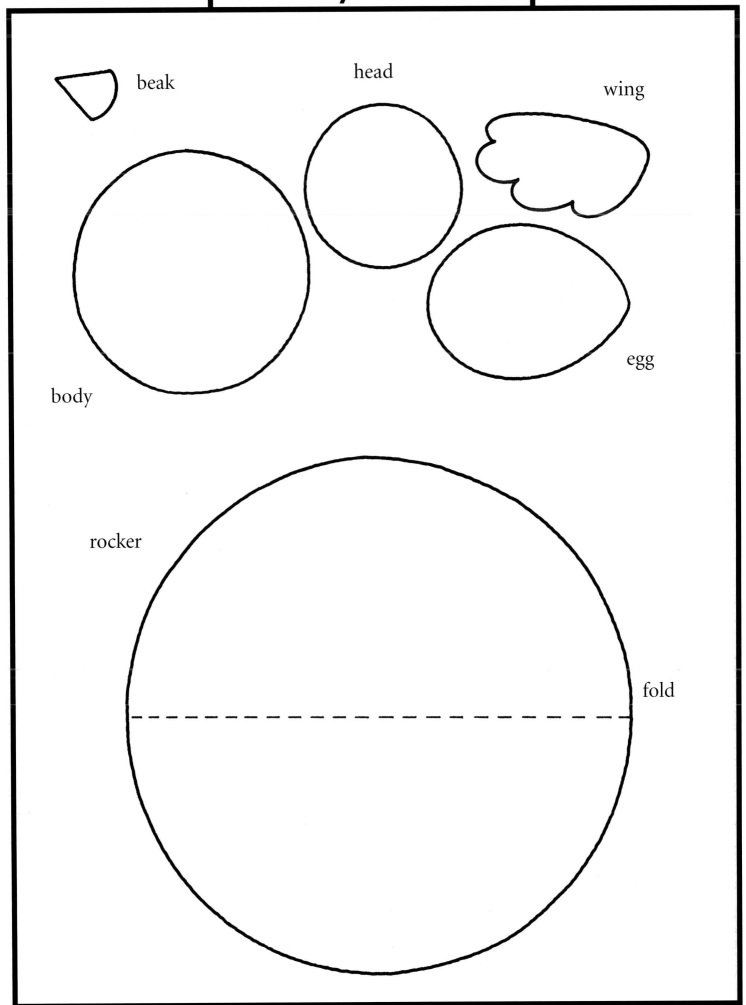

beak

head

wing

body

egg

rocker

fold

Activity sheet 14

Index

Resources list

This is a list of all of the materials needed to carry out the activities in this pack.

Writing/drawing/painting materials
- Coloured wax crayons
- Coloured pencils
- Ready-mixed paints in a range of colours
- Washable felt pens
- Paintbrushes
- Water pots

Papers (in a range of colours)
- Sugar paper
- Tissue paper
- Cartridge paper
- Shiny papers
- Crepe paper
- Filter/blotting paper
- Card
- Wallpaper

Craft/modelling/construction materials
- Safety scissors (left and right handed)
- Glue and glue brushes and PVA glue
- Sticky tape (single and double sided)
- Masking tape
- Modelling clay
- Coloured wool and ribbons
- Plastic tubs and lids
- Paper plates
- Brass fasteners
- Bubble wrap
- Plastic bottles
- Small stones/ twigs/ leaves/ conkers
- Lolly sticks
- Newspaper
- Sunflower seeds
- Sand
- Modelling tools
- Beads

Resources for investigative work
- Magnifiers
- Kitchen towel
- Honeydew melon
- Plastic straws
- Sweets
- Musical instruments
- Apples
- Compost
- Cress seeds
- Plastic/polystyrene beakers
- Plastic trays
- Cooking chocolate
- Petit-four cases
- Shoes
- Plant pot
- Teaspoons

Role-play resources
- Toy camera
- Baby clothes
- Baby doll
- Picture atlas
- Non-fiction book on the weather
- Toy phone
- Child's clothes
- Sheets/ pieces of fabric
- Globe

Other resources
- Coloured bean bags
- Large and small bowls
- 2 pence coins
- Dice
- Sieve
- Toy bricks
- Large box
- Book of Jack and the Beanstalk
- Small bats
- Large plastic container
- Toy cars
- Plastic wallets
- Cartoon video
- Guttering

6

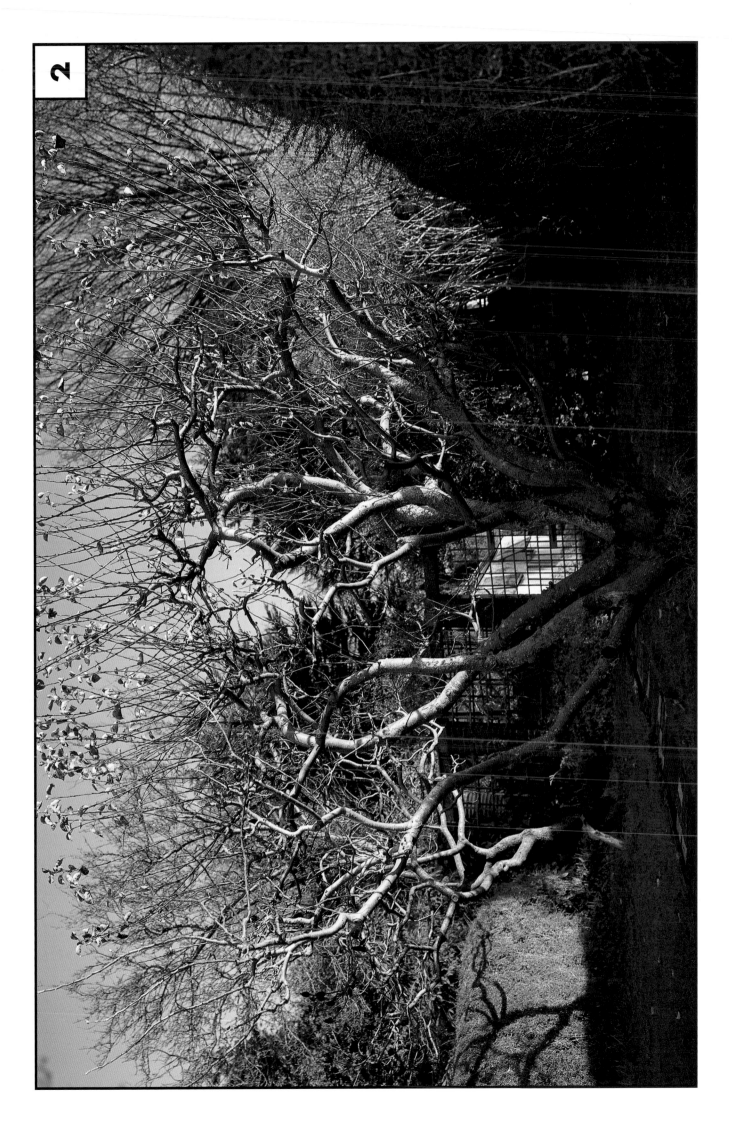